THE EPICS OF VEDVERSE

By

Vedant Phadke

THE EPICS OF VEDVERSE

#299, Kalmeshwar Galli, Kadoli, Dist - Belagavi,
Karnataka. 590 001
Cell: 89703 57947 • Email: vedantphadke28@gmail.com

First Edition
15th August 2025

Printed & Published by
R.C. Joglekar
for **Omega Publications**
Emerald Corner, Maratha Colony, Belagavi
Corespondence:
#40, Yashwant Vihar, Nanawadi, Belagavi 590 009
Email: omegapress@gmail.com
Cell : +91 988 620 3256

Cover Credits
Vedant Phadke

Layout & Pre-press
Sudhir Joglekar

Price : **Rs. 150/-**

ISBN 978-81-984518-9-7

Dedicated to the best selling authors of India

Akshat Gupta,

Amish Tripathi

&

Harsheath Chauhan

Contents

Preface by Rushikesh Bahadur Desai 5

Dream or Destiny... 7

The Call of Shimla 11

The Warning... 15

The Mohini Jungle Stay Resort 19

The Shadows in the Moonlight 24

The Patient at the Hospital... 29

The Sacrifice... 34

A Strange Personality 39

The Sacred Prophecy 44

A Prophetic Vision 49

The Trials of a Chosen warrior 54

The Passage of Quests 59

The Prestigious achievement 65

The Final Confrontation 70

Vedant Phadke's

The Epics of Vedverse

I am curious about and appreciate young people's writing for several reasons. But the main reasons, I think, are that they think in myriad different ways, distinct from us, their ways of expression, word -building, vocabulary and sentence formation are new, and joyous. The way they use language is interesting and invigorating. Picking up a book by a young author can be therapeutic, working like a de-ageing tablet.

However, the prime reason that drives me to such writers and their works, is their defiance. Defiance to what, you say - is that to societal norms?, the strict rules of what makes literature and what is not? , or the age old question as to why write? No.

It is the warning to all writers, all over the world, that was latent in the Mahabharata- the grand old tale. The voice hidden in these three words - Vyasocchishtam jagat sarvam is at once a sane voice and a silent threat. It can mean: ``Whatever anyone speaks or writes is something already spoke or written by Sage Vyasa Muni, the author of the Mahabharata". This is enough to make a pessimist put down her pen.

I am not saying today's young men and women are yet to read this. But they are quiet aware of such geriatric advice. They hear things like this everyday: ``What ever you are trying to do today, we have done it all, in worse conditions and for far less a reward!". But then, they seem to have overgrown it. That calls for courage of conviction and a goading driven by creativity. They are not disrespectful of their elders. Nor have they stopped listening to them. It is just that they feel strongly that they have something to say and that they would not let anyone stop them. What they plan to say, may be different in either content or style. But it is new and useful, if it is shared in a way that it is understood across generations.

The novella uses the technique of a story within a story. It speaks of friends who are driven by the desire to make a film that they have seen in their dreams. A series of uncanny situation lead to the interesting climax. It is racy and visually enriching with detailed accounts of nature and the inner workings of the human mind. It lets the reader experience the trip, which is the whole point of narrative story telling.

Serious writing by young people is scarce. Serious writing about music and culture is even more so. That is why, Vedant's writing seems promising. May Vedant remain true to his name. May he continue to explore and write. May he bring before us the worlds that we do not know of, or have little understood. More power to his pen!

Belgavi — *—Rishikesh Bahadur Desai*

14th June 2025 — Senior Assistant Editor, *The Hindu,* Belagavi

Dream or Destiny...

*"A dream is a whisper of fate,
but destiny is the roar of reality."*

The heavy monsoon clouds hung low over the city of Shimla, casting a shadow of somber darkness that made the normally bustling streets eerily quiet. Rain cascaded down in torrents, flooding the narrow pathways, and the distant sound of thunder added to the foreboding atmosphere. In the midst of this storm, standing tall against the elements, was an ancient temple.

The temple stood at the heart of the city, its intricate architecture a testament to centuries of history. As the rain pounded the stone walls, the glimmering silver plaque at the temple's entrance caught the eye. The plaque read:

"Shri Trilok Nath Mandir - Shimla."

Inside the temple, the air was thick with the scent of incense and age-old mystery. The walls, etched with inscriptions in a forgotten script, seemed to hum with the weight of stories untold. In the heart of the temple, within the Garbhgrah, the sanctum of the gods, stood the revered statues of the Hindu Trinity—Brahma, Vishnu, and Shiva. The rain outside only intensified the silence within, broken only by the occasional distant rumble of thunder.

Suddenly, a deafening thunderclap struck, followed by a jagged streak of lightning that illuminated the temple in an otherworldly glow. The wind howled through the temple, rattling the old wooden doors, and the bells hanging from the temple's high ceilings began to ring with an eerie, almost foretelling sound.

Outside, the storm had grown fiercer. The wind seemed to have a life of its own, howling through the trees and sending a chill down the spine of anyone caught in its path. The scene shifted quickly, now showing a dense, dark forest, where the rain fell so heavily that it blurred the line between earth and sky. The trees, ancient and towering, were bent almost horizontally in the wind, their leaves whipping around like ghosts.

In the depths of this forest, a solitary figure moved, his silhouette barely visible through the rain and mist. He carried a lantern, its dim light flickering in the storm, casting strange shadows on the ground as he walked with purpose. His appearance was that of a sage, draped in simple robes that clung to his wet skin, his hair soaked by the relentless downpour. His footsteps were steady, yet there was a hint of weariness in his stride. He was deep in thought, murmuring softly to himself as if speaking to the heavens.

"Oh Lord," the sage murmured, his voice barely audible above the howling wind. "I think I'll never find the perfect place to begin my meditation. If only I could find a place of peace, then perhaps my quest could finally come to an end."

He paused, looking around the forest, his gaze piercing the shadows. But the trees were silent, as if holding their breath.

Then, out of the darkness, a flicker of something caught his eye. Ahead, hidden among the trees and vines, was a cave—an unexpected haven in the midst of this chaotic storm. The sage quickened his pace, drawn by an inexplicable pull. He reached the cave's entrance and, for a moment, simply stood there, taking in the serenity that surrounded him. The wind had calmed, and the rain had softened, as if nature itself were welcoming him.

Stepping inside, the air was cool and dry. The sage's lantern cast long shadows against the cave walls, revealing strange markings—ancient symbols carved into the stone. But it was not the carvings that caught his attention; it was something deeper, something hidden in the shadows. There, tucked away in a cluster of overgrown bushes, was a statue—a figure that seemed out of place, almost as if it had been waiting for him.

The statue's eyes were dark, unblinking, and unyielding. But as the sage approached, something strange happened. The eyes of the statue seemed to glimmer, as if they were alive, reacting to his presence. The sage, ever the seeker of truth, felt an instinctual shiver run down his spine. He couldn't explain it, but the energy in the cave had shifted. This place, this statue, felt ancient, powerful.

Without hesitation, the sage moved to the center of the cave, cleared a small space, and sat cross-legged. He placed the lantern beside him and closed his eyes, preparing himself for the deep meditation that had eluded him for so long. Hours passed, the silence stretching on. The sage's breath grew steady, and his mind began to quiet, sinking deeper into the meditative state.

In the midst of his meditation, something inside him shifted. The deep, quiet energy of the cave seemed to stir. The air grew thicker, almost tangible. Suddenly, a sensation unlike any the sage had ever felt washed over him. His Root Chakra—the Muladhara—began to hum with energy, as if awakening from a long slumber. The sage's body tensed, his breath becoming shallow, as if he had crossed a threshold into a new realm.

At that very moment, the statue began to tremble. A low rumbling sound filled the cave, and before the sage could react, the statue cracked. The pieces split with a deafening noise, as if some ancient seal had been broken. From the shattered statue, a dark, shadowy figure emerged—its form wreathed in a smoky mist, its presence both terrifying and captivating.

The shadowy spirit locked eyes with the sage. In that instant, the spirit surged forward, its form dissolving into the sage's body with a violent rush. The sage's eyes snapped open, glowing with a menacing red light, his body now suspended in midair. His muscles contorted, and his face twisted into an expression of unimaginable horror.

A bone-chilling scream erupted from his throat, a scream that echoed through the cave and into the forest beyond. The sage's body, now no longer his own, began to transform. His limbs grew longer, his skin stretched and cracked, and his eyes burned with an unnatural fire. The transformation was quick—too quick for anyone to comprehend. The once serene sage was now a terrifying creature, its red eyes blazing like two fiery orbs.

The creature hovered in the air for a moment, howling in agony and rage. Then, with an explosion of wind and dark energy, it vanished from the cave, leaving nothing but a lingering sense of dread. But the terror didn't end there.

In the blink of an eye, the creature reappeared—standing before the viewer, its form a grotesque blend of man and monster. The force of its sudden appearance sent a jolt of fear through the heart of anyone who might be watching. And then, just as quickly as it had appeared, everything went dark.

Arjun's eyes snapped open. His breath came in quick, panicked gasps. Sweat poured down his face, and his heart pounded in his chest. The dream had been so vivid, so real. But it was just that—a dream. A horrifying, nightmarish vision. Arjun sat up in bed, his mind racing as the images of the creature, the sage, and the shattered statue lingered in his thoughts.

He rubbed his eyes, trying to shake the feeling that something was wrong. But deep down, Arjun couldn't shake the sense that this dream had a meaning—something he couldn't yet understand. And as the storm outside raged on, he knew that whatever had started in that cave was far from over.

***

The Call of Shimla

"Some places don't just call you;
they summon your very soul."

The alarm blared at 5:00 a.m., echoing faintly in the quiet apartment. Arjun groaned, rubbing his eyes as he rolled out of bed. He had barely slept, the recurring nightmare haunting him once more. It wasn't the typical jumbled imagery of bad dreams; it felt vivid, like stepping into another realm. The dense forest, the ominous cave, the eerie statue—they were too real to ignore. With a heavy sigh, he got up and freshed himself , he grabbed his yoga mat from the corner of the room and unrolled it in the middle of the floor. His routine was a refuge, a way to silence his restless mind. The stretches were deliberate, each movement smooth and controlled, as if pushing the weight of the dream out of his muscles.

By the time the clock hit 6:00 a.m., sweat dripped from his forehead, and his breaths had steadied. He folded the mat and caught a glimpse of himself in the mirror. His reflection stared back, pale and restless. "It's just a dream," he muttered, though the words felt hollow.

The sound of soft footsteps broke his train of thought. Shreyas, his roommate and best friend, stumbled out of his room, his hair a mess and his eyes half-closed. "Morning, champ," he mumbled, shuffling toward the kitchenette. The hiss of boiling water filled the air as he began brewing their morning coffee.

Arjun sat at the small dining table, his fingers drumming

on the surface. The dream replayed in his mind like a haunting melody. The sage, the glowing eyes of the statue, the transformation—it was all too much.

"You're unusually quiet this morning," Shreyas said, setting a steaming cup of coffee in front of him. "What's up? Bad dreams again?"

Arjun nodded, his jaw tight. "The same one. It's been fifteen days, Shreyas. Same dream, every single night. The forest, the cave, the statue... it's like it's trying to tell me something."

Shreyas took a sip of his coffee, studying Arjun over the rim of the cup. "You've been pushing yourself too hard. First the film, now all these expectations... maybe your brain is just fried."

"It's not just stress," Arjun snapped, then softened his tone. "I know it sounds crazy, but it feels real. Like... it's a memory, not a dream."

Shreyas leaned back in his chair, raising an eyebrow. "A past life, maybe?" he teased. Arjun didn't laugh. "I don't know. But it's driving me insane. I need answers." Shreyas shrugged. "Well, maybe it's time to take a break. Clear your head. A trip, maybe? Just the two of us."

Before Arjun could respond, his phone buzzed on the table. The screen lit up with the name: Raghunathan Films.

"It's Sir," Arjun said, his heart skipping a beat. He answered the call, his voice steady despite his unease. "Hello, Sir." The voice on the other end was brisk. "Arjun, come to the office immediately. We have something important to discuss."

"Yes, Sir. I'll be there soon," Arjun replied, already heading to his room to get ready. He took a bath , got ready in an outfit of an office guy with bag on his back. As he laced his sneakers, Shreyas called out, "Don't worry about the trip, man. By the time you're back, I'll have everything planned." Arjun gave a distracted nod, his mind already racing as he left the apartment.

The office of Raghunathan Films was a hive of activity, with assistants scurrying about and phones ringing incessantly. Arjun stepped in, greeted by the sight of posters from their biggest hits adorning the walls. He had always admired the legacy this place represented.

"Ah, Arjun!" Raghunathan's voice boomed as he emerged from his cabin. His presence was commanding, his handshake firm. "Your debut film was a masterpiece, my boy. Critics loved it, and the box office numbers don't lie. Congratulations!" "Thank you, Sir," Arjun said, bowing his head slightly.

"But there's no time to rest on your laurels," Raghunathan continued, gesturing for Arjun to follow him into his cabin. "I have a new project in mind, and I want you to direct it." Arjun sat down, intrigued. "What kind of project?" "Folklore," Raghunathan said, his eyes sparkling. "India is rich with chilling tales—legends, myths, ghost stories. I want you to bring one of them to life."

Arjun leaned forward, curiosity piqued. "Which one?"

"That's for you to decide," Raghunathan said. "But I have a suggestion: Shimla. Its haunting beauty, its dense forests... it's the perfect backdrop for a story rooted in mystery."

At the mention of Shimla, Arjun felt a shiver run down his spine. His dream flashed before him—the forest, the cave, the statue. Was this a coincidence, or was something pulling him toward Shimla? "Shimla?" he repeated, his voice barely above a whisper.

"Yes, Shimla," Raghunathan said, oblivious to Arjun's unease. "I want you to visit the place, soak in the atmosphere, and let the story find you. So, what do you say?" Arjun hesitated, the weight of the dream pressing on him. But this was an opportunity he couldn't pass up. "I'll do it," he said finally.

"Excellent!" Raghunathan clapped his hands. "I'll have my team arrange everything. You leave next week."

When Arjun returned home, he found Shreyas sprawled on

the couch, scrolling through his phone. "Guess what?" Shreyas said, a wide grin on his face. "What?" Arjun asked, his mind still on the meeting. "I've planned our trip! Pack your bags, buddy. We're going to Shimla!" Arjun froze, the color draining from his face. "Shimla?"

Shreyas nodded enthusiastically. "Yeah, it's perfect, right? A cool getaway in the hills. Just what we need to unwind."

Arjun sat down, his thoughts spiraling. Shimla. The dream, the project, the trip—everything was converging on this one place.

"Why Shimla?" he muttered, more to himself than to Shreyas. Shreyas frowned. "Why not? It's beautiful, peaceful, and far from the chaos of the city." Arjun didn't respond. He felt like a puppet, being drawn toward Shimla by unseen strings. Was it destiny, or something darker?

As Shreyas rambled on about travel plans, Arjun stared out the window, his heart heavy with dread. What was waiting for him in Shimla?

***

The Warning...

"Every shadow hides a warning, but not all warnings are heeded."

The sun dipped low over the horizon, painting the sky in hues of crimson and orange. The golden rays filtered through the window blinds, casting slanted patterns across the room where Arjun sat. His thoughts were a tangled mess, swirling with fragments of a dream he couldn't fully grasp yet couldn't forget either. Shimla. The name clung to his mind like dew on a leaf at dawn.

A sudden voice cut through the thick fog of his thoughts.

"Earth to Arjun! Hello, Mr. Angry Young Man?" Shreyas waved a hand dramatically before his friend's face.

Arjun blinked, momentarily disoriented. "What?" he asked, his voice gruff.

"I just told you the plan—Shimla trip tomorrow—and you're acting like I dropped a bombshell. What's up with that?" "Shimla?" Arjun repeated, the name tasting strange on his tongue.

"Yes, Shimla. You know, snow-capped mountains, fresh air, and aunt Mohini's fancy resort. We're staying there, by the way. Thought that would excite you." A smile flickered across Arjun's face. "Aunty Mohini owns a resort now? That's... beautiful."

"Yup. So pack your stuff. We leave tomorrow at 7 a.m. And bad news—no online booking for the bus, so we'll have to register on-site."

As Shreyas rambled on, Arjun's mind wandered back to his dream, the mysterious pull he felt toward Shimla, and a strange conviction that something awaited him there—something he wasn't ready to face.

The morning was crisp, with a gentle breeze whispering through the trees as they boarded the bus. The engine roared to life, and soon they were lumbering through the bustling streets of the city, leaving behind the familiar chaos for the promise of serenity.

The journey was long, the scenery shifting from crowded highways to vast open fields and then to the undulating landscape of the foothills. By late afternoon, the golden hues of dusk bathed the world in a warm glow. "We'll stop at Rishikesh for a night," Arjun announced, breaking the comfortable silence.

Shreyas raised an eyebrow. "Why there?" "It's on the way, and I think we need to perform a pooja. Trust me—it'll be worth it."

Shreyas shrugged. "Fine by me. Just make sure there's good food involved." They reached Rishikesh just as night descended, the city glittering with temple lights that reflected on the tranquil waters of the Ganges. The air was thick with the scent of incense and the distant chants of evening prayers.

The next morning, Arjun woke before dawn and made his way to a nearby Shiva temple. The stone steps were cold beneath his feet, and the temple was cloaked in a serene silence, broken only by the rustle of leaves. He knelt before the deity, the flickering oil lamps casting shadows on his face.

With folded hands, he whispered, "Oh Lord Shiva, please guide me. Illuminate the path I am meant to tread."

A deep sense of calm settled over him as he rose, ready to continue the journey.

The bus rumbled toward Shimla, its wheels crunching against the gravel road. The landscape was now a patchwork of lush green hills and quaint villages. Arjun leaned back in his seat, his thoughts drifting aimlessly until a voice jolted him back to reality.

"Excuse me," said a young woman standing beside him. Her hair cascaded in soft waves, and her eyes sparkled with determination. "You're in my seat."

Arjun blinked, momentarily dazed. "What?" "This is seat number 21. You're sitting in it," she repeated, her tone clipped.

Shreyas nudged him. "Bro, just switch seats. No need for drama."

But Arjun's pride flared. "I was here first," he said stubbornly. The girl crossed her arms. "Fine. But don't think for a second this is okay." She settled beside him, her annoyance palpable. Arjun tried to sneak glances at her, intrigued by her presence. "This is why I prefer trains," she muttered. "But no, the train tickets had to be full." Shreyas smirked from across the aisle. "She's got a point, bro. You need to chill."

Arjun ignored him, his mind already wandering back to the strange pull Shimla held over him.

After hours of travel, the bus finally pulled into the quaint hill station of Shimla. The air was crisp and cool, carrying the faint scent of pine. The narrow streets were lined with charming colonial-style buildings, and the distant peaks gleamed white under the afternoon sun.

Arjun dialed his aunt's number. "Aunty Mohini, it's Arjun. We've arrived."

"Arjun! My dear boy, it's been so long. I'm so glad you're here. Send me your live location, and I'll have my driver pick you up."

Fifteen minutes later, a taxi arrived. The driver confirmed their identities and loaded their luggage. The road to the resort wound through dense forests, the towering trees creating a canopy above.

The serenity was suddenly shattered when a disheveled man leaped into the path of their cab, howling like a wild animal.

"Turn back!" he screamed, his voice guttural and raw.

"If you value your lives, do not go to the woods of Shimla! Death awaits you!"

The driver jumped out, slapping the man aside with two sharp strikes. "Get lost, you lunatic!"

As they drove away, Arjun turned to the driver, his voice low but urgent. "Who was that?"

The driver sighed. "He's Pashupati. Used to work at the resort but went mad a few months after it opened. Now he prowls the area, warning people about the forest. Says it's cursed."

Arjun felt a chill run down his spine. "Cursed? Why does everything keep pointing me to Shimla?" he murmured.

The driver glanced at him in the rearview mirror. "No one knows why he says what he does, but the woods… they do have their secrets."

As the cab climbed higher into the mountains, Arjun's unease grew. The forest loomed like a shadowy sentinel, its secrets waiting to be unraveled.

***

The Mohini Jungle Stay Resort

"A place of beauty, a place of horror?"

The road twisted like a serpent through the dense Shimla forest, its curves framed by towering deodar trees whose branches formed an unbroken canopy overhead. The filtered sunlight cast shifting patterns on the windshield, creating an ethereal atmosphere that made Arjun feel as though he had crossed into another world—a timeless realm where nature reigned supreme. The cool breeze carried the scent of damp earth and pine, mingling with something ancient and inexplicable, as though the forest itself held secrets older than memory.

In the passenger seat, Arjun sat quietly, his mind burdened by the cryptic words of the madman, Pashupati. His warning had been unsettling: "The forest remembers, boy. And it never forgets." The man's wild eyes and disheveled hair haunted Arjun's thoughts like a specter. Was it just the rambling of a lunatic, or was there a kernel of truth hidden in his madness?

Shreyas, who was sitting backside, glanced at him. "Still thinking about that guy, huh?" Arjun shook his head, trying to dismiss the lingering unease. "It's nothing. Just a weird encounter."

Shreyas snorted. "This place is full of weird encounters. Welcome to Shimla." Despite his friend's light-hearted tone, Arjun couldn't shake the feeling that something profound awaited him in these woods. Shimla had always held a strange allure for him—a mysterious connection woven through dreams, fleeting signs, and now this eerie encounter. Perhaps it was destiny drawing him back.

The car finally emerged from the thick foliage, revealing a breathtaking sight: The Mohini – Jungle Stay Resort. Nestled in the heart of the forest, it was a sanctuary of rustic beauty and old-world charm. The property sprawled across a gentle slope, surrounded by majestic deodar trees whose shadows danced in the golden sunlight. Wooden cottages with intricately carved balconies and sloping slate roofs dotted the landscape, their walls stained with the patina of time.

A cobblestone pathway meandered through vibrant flower beds, leading to a koi pond where orange and white fish glided gracefully beneath the water's surface. The faint aroma of freshly brewed coffee mingled with the scent of pine, creating an atmosphere that was both invigorating and serene.

The moment the car came to a halt, a familiar voice rang out.

"Arjun!"

He turned to see a woman with salt-and-pepper hair and a radiant smile walking toward him, her arms outstretched. Mohini aunty. Memories from his childhood flooded back—her warm laughter, the comforting aroma of her cooking, and the stories she would tell by the fire on chilly Shimla evenings.

"Aunty!" Arjun exclaimed, his face lighting up as he rushed forward to embrace her. "It's been so long since we last met! I was in school back then!" "Yes, my dear boy, far too long," Mohini replied, her voice thick with emotion. She held him at arm's length, her eyes brimming with pride. "Look at you! All grown up and handsome. I should start looking for someone to take care of you."

Shreyas, who had been unloading their luggage, coughed awkwardly. Mohini turned to him with a curious look. "Hmm, and you are?" she asked. "I'm Shreyas, his roommate, but honestly, more like his brother," Shreyas said with a grin.

Mohini chuckled. "Well, Shreyas, welcome to our little paradise. Come on, let me show you to your rooms."

As they walked toward the cottages, Arjun's ears caught a heated conversation between the cook and a worker near the kitchen.

"You fool!" the cook scolded. "How many times must I tell you not to go into the forest at night? Let the driver take you home!" "But, sir," the worker protested, "there's a shortcut through the forest to my house. I'll be fine." A chill ran down Arjun's spine. He paused, his gaze lingering on the dense woods beyond the resort. The trees seemed to whisper secrets, their leaves rustling with ancient knowledge. Shaking off the sense of foreboding, he followed Mohini to their rooms.

The next morning, the trio gathered for breakfast on the open veranda overlooking the forest. The table was laden with local delicacies—steaming parathas, butter dripping from their sides, fragrant aloo sabzi, and freshly squeezed orange juice. Shreyas cracked a joke about Arjun's habit of overpacking.

"You know, Mohini ma'am," Shreyas said with mock seriousness, "Arjun packs like he's shifting his entire house. If we ever go on a trip to Mars, I'm sure he'll bring his own oxygen tanks!"

Mohini burst into laughter. "Arjun, your friend is hilarious. It must be fun having him around."

"It sure is," Arjun replied, joining the laughter.

As the conversation took a heartfelt turn, Mohini asked, "Arjun, how's life treating you these days?"

"I'm doing well, Aunty," Arjun said. "My first film was a box office success, and I'm focusing on my health too. I've taken up yoga and martial arts."

Mohini wiped a tear from her eye. "God bless you, my child. You've come such a long way after losing your parents. I still regret not being able to attend their final rites because of the lockdown."

"Aunty," Arjun said gently, "what matters is that you're here now."

Shreyas added, "He's been through a lot, but he's stronger for it."

Just then, Arjun's eyes landed on a familiar figure sitting a few tables away. It was the girl from the bus—the one who had captivated him with her beauty. Without a word, he excused himself and approached her table.

"Hey," Arjun said, sitting down across from her. "If I'm not mistaken, you're the girl from the bus, right?"

The girl looked up, startled. Her expression quickly turned defensive. "Oh, great! You followed me all the way here? Don't you have better things to do?"

Arjun raised his hands in mock surrender. "Hold on! For your information, this resort belongs to my aunt. I'm not here because of you."

She turned to glance at Mohini, who was watching the interaction with a curious smile. Realizing her mistake, the girl blushed. "Oh… I'm sorry. I jumped to conclusions."

Arjun leaned in slightly, his voice playful. "If I'd known your accusations would come with such a cute apology, I'd have followed you on purpose."

The girl's cheeks turned a deeper shade of red. "You're quite the charmer, aren't you?" she said, trying to hide her smile.

"Only when the occasion calls for it," Arjun replied, extending his hand. "I'm Arjun, by the way."

"Aditi," she said, shaking his hand.

Arjun grinned. "Nice to meet you, Aditi. You know, they say first impressions are everything. So, should I go ahead and call this a love-hate start?"

Aditi laughed despite herself, her defenses melting away.

"Let's stick to 'friends' for now."

"Friends it is," Arjun said, flashing a charming smile.

And so, amidst the lush greenery of the Mohini Jungle Stay Resort, a new connection began to blossom.

***

The Shadows in the Moonlight ...

"The moon reveals what the sun cannot—
secrets lurking in the dark."

The forest wrapped itself in an unsettling silence, broken only by the occasional rustle of leaves stirred by a frigid breeze. The towering pine trees stood like ancient sentinels, their gnarled branches clawing at the night sky. Pale moonlight spilled through the gaps in the canopy, casting elongated shadows that danced like restless spirits on the forest floor.

Kishan, a worker at the Shimla resort, trudged along the winding trail cutting through the heart of the woods. His breath emerged in white puffs, vanishing into the cold air. The path was treacherous, littered with loose stones and tangled roots that caught at his worn boots. Despite being accustomed to the journey, unease prickled at the edges of his mind tonight.

He pulled his jacket tighter around himself, but the chill that gripped him went deeper than the cold. A memory surfaced—the cook's hushed warning over dinner just a few hours ago.

"The forest is restless tonight, Kishan. Strange sounds have been heard near the northern trail. You should stay back."

Kishan had laughed it off then, dismissing the words as mere superstition. But now, with the oppressive darkness pressing in around him, those warnings echoed in his mind like a haunting refrain.

A sudden rustle broke the stillness. Kishan froze, his heart stuttering in his chest. He scanned the shadows, his eyes straining to pierce the gloom.

Nothing. Just the wind stirring the branches, or so he told himself.

He resumed his walk, quickening his pace. His heavy footfalls seemed deafening against the eerie quiet. The path twisted and turned, leading deeper into the forest.

Then he saw them—two yellow eyes glowing from the shadows ahead, unblinking and malevolent. Kishan's breath caught in his throat. The eyes didn't waver, didn't flinch. They just watched, as though waiting.

A low, guttural growl rumbled through the trees, vibrating through the cold air. Panic surged through Kishan's veins. "Stay calm," he whispered to himself, though his voice trembled. He took a tentative step backward, but a sudden blur of movement behind him made him whip around.

Shadows flickered and danced, but nothing solid met his gaze. His pulse thundered in his ears, drowning out all rational thought. "Who's there?" he called out, his voice cracking. "If this is a prank, it's not funny!"

Silence answered him, thick and suffocating. Then came the growl again, closer this time. It reverberated through the night, primal and menacing. Kishan's breath hitched as he noticed something glistening in the moonlight—a dark green liquid dripping onto the path. The soil hissed and sizzled where it touched.

Fear clamped down on his chest like a vise. He wanted to run, to flee from whatever horror lurked in the shadows, but his legs refused to obey.

A sudden movement caught his eye. Emerging from the darkness was a massive creature, its form monstrous and grotesque. It stood at least ten feet tall, with scales that shimmered dark green under the moonlight. Its lizard-like tail swayed menacingly, and its yellow eyes glowed with an almost intelligent malice.

Kishan's scream ripped through the forest as the creature

lunged, claws gleaming in the pale light.

The sun rose reluctantly over Shimla, casting a feeble light across the snow-dusted landscape. The resort nestled at the edge of the forest bustled with activity. Guests in thick coats sipped steaming cups of tea on the terrace, their laughter mingling with the crisp mountain air.

In the administrative office, Mohini, the resort manager, sat at her desk, going through the day's reports. Her brow furrowed as she read through the maintenance log. There had been complaints about strange noises from the forest side rooms.

A sudden knock on the door made her look up. The receptionist, a young woman with wide, frightened eyes, stood at the threshold.

"Madam," she said, her voice trembling, "it's Kishan. He's been found dead."

Mohini's heart skipped a beat. "What? How?"

"They're saying it was a wild animal attack." The receptionist's hands shook as she held up a photograph. "But… it's horrifying. His arm and leg are missing, and his head…" She trailed off, unable to continue.

Mohini took the photograph with trembling hands. Her breath caught in her throat as she saw the image. The mutilation was beyond anything she'd ever seen. Deep claw marks marred the ground where his body had been found.

As she struggled to process the information, Arjun, entered the office. His sharp features were etched with concern.

"I overheard," he said quietly. "What happened to Kishan?" Mohini hesitated before handing him the photograph. Arjun's eyes widened as he took in the gruesome scene. "This isn't a normal animal attack," he said, his voice low. "The bite marks… they're too large for any known predator."

Mohini's lips pressed into a thin line. "We need to inform

the forest department. They have to investigate this." Arjun nodded, but unease gnawed at him. Memories of his recurring nightmares surfaced—visions of a monstrous creature with glowing eyes and razor-sharp claws. Could it be the same one?

Later, as he sat alone in the lounge, the pieces of the puzzle began to fit together. The strange warnings from the cook, the cryptic words of the madman Pashupati, and now Kishan's brutal death—it all pointed to something far beyond mere coincidence.

Mohini found him lost in thought. "Arjun," she said gently, "you've been quiet all day. Is something bothering you?" He hesitated before speaking. "I don't know, Aunt Mohini. It's as if these incidents are connected. It feels like they're trying to tell me something." She placed a comforting hand on his shoulder. "Sometimes, strange things happen for a reason. Trust in God's plan, Arjun. He'll guide you."

Her warmth eased the turmoil in his mind. "Thank you, Aunt Mohini. You're like a mother to me." She smiled. "And I'll always be here for you."

That evening, as Arjun wandered the resort's guest corridor, a raised voice caught his attention. He peeked through a slightly ajar door to see Aditi, her face flushed with anger as she argued on the phone.

"I can't believe you're canceling!" she snapped. "You promised you'd be here."

She hung up abruptly, storming out of the room, only to find Arjun standing there. Her eyes narrowed. "Were you eavesdropping on me? One day of friendship, and you're already stalking me?"

"No, no, it's not like that!" Arjun stammered, holding up his hands. "I just… heard you arguing and thought you might need someone to talk to."

After a moment of awkward silence, Aditi sighed. "Some friends bailed on me. I was counting on them, and now I'm stuck here alone."

Arjun's expression softened. "Well, if you're feeling lonely, I'd be happy to keep you company. This resort has a lot to offer, and I promise you won't be bored."

She raised an eyebrow. "And why should I trust you?"

"Because," he said with a mischievous grin, "I'm an excellent tour guide. Plus, I guarantee I'll make this vacation unforgettable."

After a beat, Aditi couldn't help but laugh. "Fine. But if you bore me, you're buying me dinner."

"Deal," he said, extending his hand.

As she turned to leave, her foot slipped on the polished floor. Before she could fall, Arjun caught her in his arms, steadying her.

"See? I've got you," he said, his voice low and charming.

Aditi blushed, her cheeks turning a delicate shade of pink. "Thanks," she mumbled, avoiding his gaze.

With a smile, he gestured toward the cafeteria. "Shall we?"

As they walked together, the mysterious shadows of Shimla seemed to fade, replaced by the blossoming warmth of newfound companionship.

***

The Patient at the Hospital...

"Not all wounds are visible, and not all patients are meant to be saved."

The morning mist lingered over the lush grounds of the Woodland Retreat Resort, a thick blanket that softened the view of the distant forest. Tall pines stood as silent sentinels, their branches swaying gently in the crisp mountain breeze. The faint chirping of unseen birds mingled with the occasional rustle of leaves, creating a tranquil symphony that could calm even the most restless soul.

On the resort's open Community hall, Arjun and Aditi sat on the sofa placed in the hall , their hands curled around steaming cups of hot chocolate. The aroma of fresh egg omelets and toasted brown bread wafted from the table before them, blending with the cool air. Aditi's gaze wandered to the vast landscape stretching beyond the manicured garden, her eyes sparkling with wonder.

"This place is magical," she said, taking a sip from her cup. "I can see why people would want to come here just to escape."

Arjun leaned back, a relaxed smile playing on his lips. "Aunt Mohini put her heart and soul into this place. It wasn't easy, but she made it happen."

Aditi turned her curious gaze to him. "And what about you, Mr. Mysterious? Where do you live, and what do you do?"

He chuckled softly, the sound warm and genuine. "I live in Mumbai, Borivali to be exact. I'm a film director by profession. My last movie, The Heavenly Waters, did pretty well at the box office. When I'm not directing, I practice martial arts. It helps me stay focused."

Her eyes widened in admiration. "A filmmaker and a martial artist? That's an unusual combination. Truly fascinating!" "Well," Arjun shrugged, "life's more interesting when you keep it unpredictable."

Before Aditi could respond, a cheerful voice interrupted them. "How are you two lovebirds doing?" Mohini called out as she approached, her face radiating warmth. Aditi's face turned pink. "Oh, no, we're not—"

Mohini waved her hand dismissively. "Relax, I'm just teasing. You kids look like you're having a good time."

Before the conversation could continue, Shreyas bounded onto the veranda, his mischievous grin firmly in place. He clapped a hand on Arjun's shoulder. "Aditi, let me warn you," he declared theatrically, "this charmer here has half the girls in our apartment complex swooning over him. They practically fight over whose balcony he waves at first!"

Everyone burst into laughter, and Aditi blushed furiously, hiding her face behind her cup.

Late that night, the atmosphere around the resort had taken on a different tone. The cheerful bustle of guests had given way to an eerie silence. The fog thickened, and the cold was biting, seeping through layers of clothing.

Aman, one of the guests, decided to take a leisurely walk along the resort's perimeter after dinner. His heavy meal weighed on him, and he stretched his arms, speaking to himself.

"A little walk after all that food sounds perfect."

His footsteps crunched against the gravel path as he scrolled through social media on his phone, the blue light illuminating his face. The resort's lights faded into the background as he ventured farther from the main building.

Suddenly, a distant howl pierced the night, making him freeze mid-step. His brows furrowed. "Did I just hear something?" he muttered. "Ah, probably my imagination."

He shook his head and continued walking, but unease clung to him like a second skin. The fog grew denser, curling around the trees like ghostly fingers. The cold intensified, biting at his skin.

Another howl echoed, this one closer, sharper. A chill ran down Aman's spine. He quickened his pace, trying to shake off the creeping dread.

A low growl stopped him in his tracks. This time, the sound was unmistakably near. Sweat beaded on his forehead despite the freezing air. Slowly, he turned, his breath catching in his throat.

Standing just a few feet away was a massive beast. Its glowing yellow eyes pierced through the fog, locking onto Aman. The creature stood over ten feet tall, its scales glistening dark green under the pale moonlight. Its muscular body resembled a lizard's, but its hands were eerily human, ending in sharp claws. Jagged teeth gleamed under its snarling mouth, and a long, whip-like tail swayed menacingly behind it.

Aman screamed, stumbling backward. The creature roared, shaking the ground beneath them. Desperate, Aman grabbed a fallen branch, frantically setting it alight with his lighter to create a makeshift torch. As the monster lunged, he hurled the flaming stick at its face.

The beast howled in pain, its claws swiping wildly before retreating into the shadows. Aman panted heavily, his legs trembling as he limped toward the faint lights of Shimla. His strength waned, and he collapsed near the outskirts.

The next evening, Mohini paced her office, her face etched with worry. "This isn't normal," she muttered, discussing Kishan's death with the resort manager. "It's no longer safe for anyone to venture into the forest. We have to warn our guests immediately."

Before she could continue, her phone buzzed. It was Mr. Rana, the forest officer. His voice was urgent.

"Mrs. Mohini, one of your guests, a young man named Aman, has been admitted to the hospital. He was found unconscious near the forest by our patrolling team. He's injured but stable for now."

Mohini's face paled. "What? Injured? Oh my God. We'll be there immediately," she said, grabbing her keys.

Outside, Arjun sat on a bench, sipping tea. Seeing his aunt's distressed expression, he hurried over.

"Aunt Mohini, what's wrong?" "There's an emergency," she said, her voice trembling. "One of our guests has been attacked. We need to get to the hospital now."

At the hospital, the scene was grim. Aman lay unconscious, his leg bandaged and covered in claw marks. Mr. Rana stood by the bed, his expression grave. "Our team found him near the forest's edge," he explained. "He was injured and muttering something about a monster before he passed out. This isn't the work of a regular animal. Whatever it was, it's dangerous."

Arjun's eyes darkened as he examined the claw marks. His mind raced. Could this be the creature from his dreams?

Driving back to the resort, Mohini's voice trembled. "Arjun, I built this resort after so much hardship. After your Uncle Sudhir's death, this was my way of keeping his memory alive. But now, I don't think we'll survive another year."

Arjun placed a reassuring hand on her shoulder. "Don't worry, Aunt Mohini. We'll figure this out. Maybe it's just a panther or some other animal. Let's not jump to conclusions."

But deep inside, Arjun couldn't shake the nagging feeling that this was something far more sinister.

Suddenly, a figure darted onto the road. Arjun slammed the brakes, the car skidding to a halt. It was Pashupati, the madman from the village.

"I warned you!" he bellowed, his eyes wild. "This land is cursed! The banyan tree, the holy guardian, was felled for your greed. Now the forest's protector has awakened, and it will not rest until it claims what's owed. More will die! The screams of the innocent will echo through these woods!"

Arjun's patience snapped. He leapt out of the car, grabbing Pashupati by the collar. "Enough of your nonsense!" he shouted, delivering a punch. Mohini pulled him back. "Arjun! Stop! He's not worth it."

Pashupati staggered away, laughing maniacally. "You cannot escape the forest's wrath," he yelled, disappearing into the shadows.

Arjun clenched his fists, his resolve hardening. "Aunt Mohini, we're going into the forest tonight. It's time to find out what's really happening."

***

The Sacrifice...

"To gain something truly valuable, one must be ready to lose everything."

The wind hissed through the towering trees, carrying with it a bone-chilling cold that seemed to seep into every crevice of the forest. Moonlight fought to pierce through the dense canopy, but the ancient branches stood firm, casting tangled shadows on the ground. The whispers of rustling leaves intertwined with distant cries of nocturnal creatures, creating a symphony that spoke of something ominous.

The resort stood at the forest's edge, a haven for those seeking tranquility amidst nature. Tonight, however, it was a prison of dread. Inside the community hall, a heavy silence gripped the air. Arjun sat rigidly in his chair, his brows furrowed in concentration. Beside him, his best friend Shreyas, usually the life of any gathering, stared blankly at the floor, his face pale with disbelief. Aditi, still trembling from the horrors she had witnessed in the forest, clutched her arms tightly around herself. Mohini, Arjun's aunt and the owner of the resort, sat with her hands folded on the table, her face shadowed by guilt and sorrow.

The tension was palpable, thick enough to choke on. Arjun finally broke the silence, his voice steady but laced with urgency. "Before Aunt Mohini says anything, I request everyone to keep this discussion among us." His eyes flickered with determination. "Aunty, what was that lunatic talking about? Which Banyan tree?"

Mohini sighed, the weight of years pressing down on her shoulders. Her voice was heavy with remorse. "After Sudhir's death(her husband), I was shattered. I couldn't see a way forward. But one of my old friends encouraged me to start fresh, to rebuild. With my son's help, we found this location and began constructing the resort here, right in the heart of the forest."

Her gaze drifted toward the window, where shadows danced under the faint moonlight. "Before the resort was built, there was an ancient, sacred Banyan tree. It was tied with a holy thread, a symbol of reverence. It had stood here for centuries, untouched by time. But in my eagerness to create something new, I made the decision to cut the tree down. I thought no harm would come of it." Her voice cracked. "I believed it was the right thing to do for the future of this resort... but I fear now that my actions have awakened something terrible. Something that has been harming my guests."

Silence followed her confession, broken only by the distant howl of the wind. Arjun's jaw clenched, his knuckles turning white as he gripped the edge of the table. "Aunt, unknowingly you have done a great wrong by disturbing something ancient. This... this force, whatever it is, is a great threat."

He paused, his mind racing with fragmented memories of the vivid dreams that had haunted him since his arrival at the resort—dreams that now seemed all too real. "I have to dig deeper into this. There's more to this than we realize."

Shreyas, his voice steady despite the fear in his eyes, spoke up. "We need to go into the forest tonight. We need to confront whatever is causing this."

Arjun nodded, already formulating a plan. "I'll call Mr. Rana, the forest officer. We need his help."

He pulled out his phone and dialed the number. "Mr. Rana," he said as soon as the call connected, "we need you and your team here. Something's wrong in these woods. We need to investigate it tonight."

Mr. Rana's voice was grim. "I'll be there with my officers. Stay inside until we arrive."

The forest loomed before them like a living, breathing entity. The path that once seemed inviting was now a twisted corridor of shadows. Arjun, Shreyas, Mr. Rana, and a team of armed officers stood at the edge, their flashlights slicing through the darkness.

"Stay close," Mr. Rana instructed. "No one wanders off."

The group moved cautiously, each step echoing through the eerie silence. The smell of damp earth and decaying leaves filled the air. The trees seemed to lean closer, their gnarled branches like skeletal fingers reaching for the intruders.

Arjun's heart raced as he scanned the darkness. His mind was sharp, his senses heightened by the adrenaline coursing through his veins. Every rustle, every shadow was a potential threat.

A sudden howl pierced the air, sending chills down their spines. Arjun froze. It was the same sound he had heard in his dreams. His eyes darted toward a nearby bush that trembled unnaturally.

"Stay alert!" Mr. Rana commanded. The officers raised their weapons, their fingers poised on the triggers. The tension was suffocating. Then, without warning, a scream shattered the silence. One of the officers was gone—vanished into the darkness.

Panic gripped the group. Arjun's instincts kicked in. "Form a circle! Watch each other's backs!" he shouted.

The creature struck again, a blur of movement and glowing yellow eyes. It was a grotesque being, towering and monstrous, with claws that gleamed in the faint light. Its growl was guttural, filled with primal rage.

Arjun ducked as it lunged at him, its claws slicing through

the air. He retaliated with a swift kick, sending it stumbling backward. The fight was a blur of adrenaline and survival. Arjun moved with precision, each strike calculated.

But the creature was relentless. It lunged again, its claws aimed at Arjun's chest. Shreyas, seeing his friend in danger, acted without thinking.

"Arjun! No!" he shouted, pushing him out of the way.

Time seemed to slow as the creature's claws raked across Shreyas's chest. Blood sprayed into the air as he collapsed to the ground. Arjun's heart shattered.

"Shreyas!" he screamed, dropping to his knees beside his friend. "Stay with me! Please!" Shreyas's breathing was labored, his face pale. He managed a weak smile. "Arjun... it's okay. You've always been there for me. It's my turn now. Finish this... for all of us."

His eyes closed, and his body went still. "No!" Arjun's cry echoed through the forest. Tears blurred his vision as grief consumed him. But even in his sorrow, rage burned in his chest.

The creature, sensing his fury, hesitated. Arjun seized the moment. With a primal scream, he charged at it, his fists flying. The monster roared in defiance but retreated, vanishing into the shadows.

Arjun collapsed, his strength spent. Darkness crept at the edges of his vision until it finally claimed him.

The first rays of dawn filtered through the trees, casting a pale light over the resort. Arjun opened his eyes, disoriented and weak. He was back in the community hall, with Mohini and Aditi by his side.

"Arjun, thank God you're awake," Aditi said, her voice thick with emotion. Her eyes were red from crying.

Mohini's face was etched with sorrow. "I'm so sorry, Arjun. I never meant for any of this to happen." Arjun sat up abruptly.

"Where's that bloody creature? Who killed my best friend?!" His voice broke, filled with anguish. "I'll never let it go..."

Aditi placed a hand on his shoulder. "Arjun, please calm down. We're all heartbroken over Shreyas. But we have to accept that it's over." "No," Arjun said, his voice steely with resolve. "It's not over. I will finish this. I will destroy that creature, no matter the cost."

***

A Strange Personality

"Sometimes, the strangest souls hide the deepest wisdom."

The morning sun bathed Mohini Jungle Stay Resort in hues of gold, casting long shadows over dew-kissed foliage. The thick mist that had clung stubbornly to the forest all night now slithered away like a retreating army, revealing a landscape teeming with life. Vibrant flowers adorned the neatly arranged beds around the cottages, their petals swaying gently in the crisp breeze. Birds chirped jubilantly, their melodies rising and falling like notes of an intricate symphony.

The serene scene, however, did little to comfort Arjun.

He stood by the large bay window of his cottage, his hands clenched at his sides. His eyes, bloodshot from a restless night, gazed at the endless stretch of forest. The memories of the previous day clung to him like a persistent shadow—Shreyas' laughter during their carefree days in Mumbai, their shared victories on the cricket field, and wild late-night parties filled with jokes and music.

But now those joyful memories were marred by the image of Shreyas' lifeless body, sprawled on the forest floor, eyes frozen in a gaze that spoke of terror and pain. A tear trembled at the edge of Arjun's eye. He quickly wiped it away, unwilling to let the grief consume him.

A soft knock at the door pulled him from his torment.

Aditi entered quietly, her expression clouded with concern. Her soft features, usually radiant with a smile, were now drawn with worry. Her hair was tied back in a messy bun, and she wore a simple beige kurta paired with jeans, her usual charm replaced by a somber demeanor.

"Arjun," she called gently, "are you okay?"

He forced a smile, but his voice was hollow. "Yeah, I'm fine. What could possibly happen to me?"

Aditi's eyes softened. She could see through his facade—the brittle edge in his tone, the way his shoulders sagged under the weight of sorrow. She walked up to him and placed a hand on his shoulder. "It's okay to let it out," she whispered. "I know you're hurting. Shreyas meant a lot to you… to all of us. It's not easy to lose someone like that."

Her words pierced the dam Arjun had built around his emotions. His face crumpled as he pulled her into a hug, his sobs breaking the silence. "That monster… that monster killed my brother," he choked out. "I won't let it get away with this. I swear I'll send it to hell."

Aditi's own eyes glistened, but she held back her tears. "Arjun, I know it's painful. But Shreyas wouldn't want you to give up. He sacrificed himself so you could live. Be strong—for him. We'll face this together." Arjun stepped back, his breathing ragged. He wiped his face, determination flickering in his eyes. "You're right. I can't let this defeat me. It's time to end this once and for all."

Before either of them could speak further, there was another knock at the door. Mohini, the resort manager, stood at the entrance. Her crisp white sari was immaculate, though her face bore lines of fatigue.

"Arjun," she said, "Dr. Vaani has arrived. She's waiting in the lobby."

Dr. Vaani was an imposing figure. Her curly hair was tied into a neat bun, and she wore a practical olive-green jacket over a pair of cargo pants. A rugged backpack hung over her shoulder, hinting at years of fieldwork. Her sharp eyes gleamed with intelligence and curiosity, tempered by a calm demeanor that seemed unshakable.

As Arjun and Aditi greeted her, she immediately sensed the tension hanging over them.

"Dr. Vaani, thank you for coming on such short notice," Arjun said, his voice steady but strained.

"I'm here to help," she assured him. "Mohini told me you're dealing with something… unusual. Why don't you start from the beginning?" Arjun took a deep breath and recounted everything—the resort's mysterious history, the holy banyan tree, the attacks, and Shreyas' tragic death. He described the strange dreams that had plagued him and the inexplicable pull he felt toward Shimla.

Dr. Vaani listened intently, her brow furrowing with each revelation. When Arjun finished, a heavy silence hung in the room.

"It sounds like you're dealing with a Brahmarakshas," she finally said.

"A Brahmarakshas?" Aditi repeated, confusion evident in her voice.

"Yes," Dr. Vaani explained. "Brahmarakshasas are cursed beings—souls of scholars or sages who committed grave sins. Their knowledge makes them powerful, but their curse makes them vengeful. Cutting the holy banyan tree may have disturbed such a being, trapping it in a state of rage."

Arjun's face hardened. "How do we stop it?"

Dr. Vaani's gaze was grave. "That's not going to be easy. Such entities are deeply connected to ancient energies. We need to find the source of its curse and sever that bond. Tell me more about these dreams you've been having."

Arjun hesitated, then said, "I keep seeing a temple in

Shimla and a sage who transforms into a monster. Do you think they're connected?"

Dr. Vaani's eyes gleamed with realization. "The temple in your dreams might be the Shri Trilok Nath Mandir in Shimla. It's known for its inscriptions and statues of Brahma, Vishnu, and Shiva that symbolize unity and strength. The inscriptions, discovered centuries ago near the Giri River, are said to contain hidden truths. Your dreams may be guiding you to uncover those truths."

Mohini stepped forward. "We have a vehicle ready. I can drive you all to Shimla."

The group set off, their journey taking them through winding roads that meandered past verdant valleys and towering pine trees. The landscape was breathtaking, but a heavy silence lingered in the car.

Even Aditi, who usually found joy in nature's beauty, remained lost in thought.

When they arrived at the temple, it was a magnificent sight. Perched against the backdrop of snow-capped peaks, the Shri Trilok Nath Mandir stood tall and proud, its stone walls adorned with intricate carvings that glowed golden in the afternoon sunlight. The air thrummed with an ancient energy, as though the very stones remembered the passage of time.

Inside, the walls were covered in inscriptions written in an ancient script. Dr. Vaani examined them closely, her fingers tracing the faded characters.

"These are written in a rare dialect," she murmured. "We'll need an archaeologist to decode them."

A sudden, raspy voice interrupted her. "Perhaps I can help."

Startled, the group turned to see an old man standing at the temple's entrance. He was wrapped in a tattered shawl, his dark skin weathered by time and the elements. His beard was uneven, and a deep scar ran across his forehead, from which a trickle of dark crimson emerged. The acrid scent of ancient wounds clung to him, unsettling everyone.

What struck them most was his height—he towered over them, seemingly 8 to 9 feet tall.

"Who are you?" Arjun demanded, his voice edged with suspicion. The man's voice was deep and resonant, like the tolling of a bell. "Just a wanderer who knows the language of these inscriptions. I've spent my life studying them."

Dr. Vaani narrowed her eyes. "Why would you help us?"

A faint smile tugged at the corners of the man's mouth. "Because what you're dealing with concerns more than just you. And I am aware of the hardships you've faced. I am a wanderer seeking redemption for the sins of a lifetime and answers to questions only the gods dare to ask."

Arjun's instincts screamed that the man was no ordinary wanderer. Was he a savior or someone with his own hidden agenda?

As the group exchanged wary glances, the man approached the inscriptions. His fingers traced the ancient script with a familiarity that suggested he wasn't lying.

Vaani, unable to contain her curiosity, thought to herself, Is he some kind of Aghori or a Naga sadhu?

Arjun and Aditi remained astonished by the man's height and aura, torn between wariness and hope.

***

The Sacred Prophecy

"A prophecy is neither a gift nor a curse —it is a burden of truth."

The air was crisp and fresh, carrying the scent of damp soil and wildflowers. Tall cedar and pine trees formed a towering wall on either side of the path, their branches entwining to form a natural canopy that filtered the sunlight into shimmering fragments. The dense forest was alive with the rustle of leaves and the occasional chirp of birds hidden high above.

The old man led the group through the winding trail, his towering frame moving with a surprising grace that defied his age. He wore a weathered cloak that seemed to blend seamlessly with the earthy tones of the forest. His silver hair, tied in a loose knot, glinted in the dappled sunlight.

Aditi quickened her pace to walk beside him, her curiosity getting the better of her. "Sir," she asked cautiously, "may we know your name?"

The old man chuckled softly, a sound that resonated like the low rumble of distant thunder. "What's in a name, my child? A name is but a label. Let us focus on the journey."

Arjun, walking slightly behind, frowned. "He's not going to tell us, is he?" he muttered under his breath.

Dr. Vaani, the eldest member of the group and a historian with a keen eye for detail, observed the man carefully. His agile movements, confident demeanor, and enigmatic refusal to reveal his identity only deepened her suspicions. She couldn't shake the feeling that there was more to him than met the eye.

The sound of rushing water grew louder as they advanced. The path widened, revealing a breathtaking sight that made them stop in their tracks. A magnificent waterfall cascaded down rugged rocks, sparkling like liquid diamonds under the midday sun. The water tumbled into a crystal-clear lake surrounded by vibrant wildflowers. Mist rose from the base of the falls, creating shimmering rainbows in the sunlight.

Near the edge of the lake, nestled among ancient trees, stood a modest hut made of bamboo and thatch. Smoke curled from a small chimney, blending with the mist from the waterfall.

"Welcome to my humble abode," the old man announced, gesturing toward the hut.

The group stared in awe at the picturesque setting. The tranquility of the place seemed almost otherworldly, soothing their frayed nerves after the arduous trek.

The old man led them inside the hut, which was sparsely furnished but impeccably clean. A wooden table held an assortment of fresh fruits, and a kettle simmered over a small fire. The scent of boiling herbs wafted through the room, adding to the cozy atmosphere.

"Please, make yourselves comfortable," he said, handing each of them a bowl of freshly cut fruit. He poured steaming hot water into clay cups and placed them on the table. "Eat and drink. You've had a long journey."

They ate in silence, the sweet and tangy fruits refreshing their spirits. The warmth of the herbal tea seeped into their bones, chasing away the chill of the forest.

The old man finally sat down, his piercing eyes studying each of them in turn. The flickering firelight cast shadows on his weathered face, giving him an almost mythical appearance.

"Now," he began, his voice low and melodic, "let me tell you what the inscriptions on the temple walls reveal."

The old man's voice carried the weight of centuries as he

spoke, drawing the group into the depths of an ancient tale.

"Long ago, during the time of the Mahabharata, the land you now call Shimla was known as Shamli, named after Goddess Kaali. It was a place of unparalleled beauty and deep spirituality. People lived in harmony, worshipping the goddess with unwavering devotion.

"In those days, there was a wandering sage named Muni-Ratnam. A man of great wisdom, he traveled far and wide, seeking the perfect place for meditation. One day, he stumbled upon a lush cave hidden deep within the forest. The cave exuded a divine energy, and Muni-Ratnam decided it was the ideal place to begin his penance."

The group listened intently, the old man's vivid narration transporting them to an ancient world.

"One fateful evening," he continued, "as the sage meditated, a hidden statue buried in the bushes outside the cave began to tremble. The statue, ancient and forgotten, suddenly cracked open, releasing a dark shadow that surged toward the unsuspecting sage.

"The shadow entered his body, and an unnatural transformation began. His once-serene face twisted in agony as his limbs elongated, his skin darkened, and his features mutated into something monstrous. His cries echoed through the forest, a chilling reminder of his descent into darkness."

The old man's voice grew quieter, almost reverent. "That was the birth of the creature."

Arjun, who had been silent until now, interjected, "I've seen this… in my dreams. The statue, the shadow, the transformation… I didn't realize it was the same story as the inscriptions."

The old man nodded gravely. "Your dreams are more than mere visions. They are echoes of the past, guiding you toward your destiny."

The flickering firelight cast long shadows across the room as the old man continued.

"As the creature began to wreak havoc, people started disappearing," he said. "The locals were paralyzed with fear, helpless against its wrath. News of the creature eventually reached Ashwatthama, who was patrolling the neighboring states of Hastinapur.

"The villagers, desperate for salvation, begged Ashwatthama for help. After much contemplation, he devised a plan. He planted a holy banyan tree at the forest's edge and tied it with a sacred thread, creating a boundary the creature could not cross. He warned the villagers never to disturb the tree, for it was their only protection."

"But wasn't there a way to destroy the creature permanently?" Aditi asked, leaning forward.

The old man's gaze grew distant. "Ashwatthama believed there was, but it required a sacrifice. He explained that only a pure soul—one who had surrendered completely to God and lived selflessly—could give their life to create a weapon capable of destroying the creature.

"The villagers identified a man named Damodar, a devout follower of Goddess Kaali. An orphan with no family, he willingly offered his life for the greater good."

The old man's voice softened as he described the scene. "Damodar's sacrifice was not in vain. Ashwatthama used his bones to forge a powerful weapon—a holy knife, which he concealed deep within a lake. He prophesied that one day, the banyan tree would be removed, unleashing the creature once more. But he also foretold that a hero would rise to defeat it." The old man finished his tale, and a heavy silence settled over the group. The only sound was the gentle roar of the waterfall in the background. "So where is the weapon?" asked Arjun. The old man said , "Ashwathama has kept it somewhere near the lake called Suraj Tal."

Arjun broke the silence. "Where is this lake? Where is the weapon?" The old man met his gaze. "The lake is known as Suraj Tal. It lies high in the mountains, treacherous and unforgiving. But if you wish to end this, you must retrieve the weapon."

Dr. Vaani looked skeptical. "The journey to Suraj Tal is dangerous. Are you certain the weapon is still there?"

"The weapon's power ensures it remains undisturbed," the old man replied. "But retrieving it will not be easy. The path is fraught with challenges, and the creature will not sit idly by."

***

A Prophetic Vision

"What is foreseen cannot be unseen, and what is destined cannot be undone."

It was well past midnight. The resort lay enveloped in stillness, with only the occasional rustle of leaves disturbed by the chilly wind. The forest beyond the resort was a dark silhouette against the night sky, where stars blinked faintly. The clock inside the room struck three, its soft chime barely audible against the oppressive silence.

Arjun lay in his bed, his breathing slow and steady. Moonlight streamed through the half-open window, casting silvery patterns on the floor. The cold night breeze swept into the room, carrying with it an eerie, unexplainable chill. As the wind brushed against Arjun's face, his body tensed. His peaceful expression contorted as though he were grappling with something unseen.

A sudden shiver coursed through his body. His fists clenched, and he writhed as if struggling to break free from invisible chains.

Then came the dream.

Arjun found himself submerged in a vast, otherworldly lake. The water was neither warm nor cold, but its touch was unsettling. Darkness loomed all around him, thick and suffocating. Yet directly in front of him shone a piercing green light, cutting through the blackness like a beacon.

The source of the light was a colossal lotus that floated on the surface of the lake, its petals shimmering with an ethereal glow. Arjun's breath caught in his throat. There was something magnetic about the lotus, an inexplicable pull that urged him forward.

He waded toward it, his movements slow and labored as though the water resisted him. As he drew closer, the brilliance of the green light intensified, pricking his eyes like tiny shards of glass. He squinted, trying to shield his gaze, but the light was relentless.

Through the blinding radiance, he discerned the faint outline of something resting atop the lotus. A weapon. It shimmered with a divine aura—a blade of unparalleled craftsmanship, with intricate carvings that seemed to dance in the light. Beside it lay a bow, its surface gleaming with ancient energy.

Arjun's heart raced. This was no ordinary weapon; it was the stuff of legends, the kind that sages spoke of in hushed tones. He knew, deep in his bones, that this was the key to ending the terror that plagued Shimla.

With trembling hands, he reached for the weapon.

But before his fingers could graze its surface, a force struck him square in the chest. He was hurled backward, his body spiraling through the water. Pain radiated through his chest as he landed with a splash.

Gasping for breath, he looked up.

A shadowy figure had emerged in front of the lotus. Its form was indistinct, shifting like smoke in the wind. But its eyes—two burning embers—glared at him with unbridled rage. The figure let out a deafening roar, the sound reminiscent of a lion's feral cry.

Arjun's blood turned to ice. His body trembled, not from the cold but from an instinctual fear that gnawed at the edges of his mind.

The shadow advanced, its presence oppressive and suffocating. Arjun tried to move, but his limbs felt like lead.

Then, suddenly, a blinding beam of light descended from the heavens, illuminating the lake. The brilliance was otherworldly, pure and untouchable. Arjun shielded his eyes as the light took form—an ethereal figure bathed in golden radiance.

A voice, deep and commanding, echoed through the lake.

"O Keeper of the Weapon, this man is destined to be its bearer. Let him embrace his destiny and vanquish the terror of darkness."

The moment the voice faded, the shadowy figure let out a final, anguished roar before dissolving into the air. The oppressive darkness lifted, leaving only the serene glow of the lotus.

Arjun, gasping for breath, rose to his feet. His gaze locked onto the weapon once more. This time, there was no resistance. He stepped forward, his resolve unshakable, and lifted the blade and bow from the lotus. A surge of energy coursed through his veins, igniting a fire within him.

The lake shimmered and dissolved around him, and in the blink of an eye, he found himself standing at the edge of the forest near Shimla. The towering trees loomed like ancient sentinels, their branches whispering secrets to the wind. Arjun's triumph was short-lived. A chilling howl pierced the night—a sound he knew all too well. His heart clenched. The creature. The same monstrous entity that had taken Shreyas from him.

The forest trembled as the beast emerged from the shadows, its monstrous form illuminated by the pale moonlight. Its eyes glowed with malevolent fury, and its sharp teeth gleamed like daggers.

With a deafening roar, it lunged at Arjun.

Arjun braced himself, the weapon gleaming in his hand. But before he could strike, a blur of motion intercepted the creature. There was a thunderous impact as the beast was hurled backward, crashing into the trees.

Arjun's eyes widened in shock. Standing in the shadows was a man of towering height. His presence was both commanding and enigmatic. A gem on his forehead glowed with a blissful yellow light, casting a halo around him. He held a wooden staff in his hand, its surface etched with ancient symbols.

The man turned to Arjun, his voice deep and reassuring. "You are on the right path, my child. Believe in yourself. You are closer to your destiny than you realize."

Before Arjun could respond, the man vanished into the shadows, leaving only the faint glow of the gem lingering in the air.

Arjun's eyes snapped open. His chest heaved, and beads of sweat clung to his forehead. He sat up, his heart racing. The room was bathed in the soft glow of dawn. The clock on the wall read 6:30 a.m.

He rubbed his face, trying to make sense of the vivid dream—or was it more than a dream? The memory of the shadowy figure and the mysterious man with the glowing gem was etched into his mind.

After a quick shower, Arjun dressed and made his way to the resort's canteen. The aroma of freshly brewed tea filled the air, mingling with the scent of warm bread. He poured himself a cup and walked toward the community hall, seeking solace in the tranquil morning.

Dr. Vaani and Aditi were deep in conversation near the entrance. Their animated gestures and bright smiles suggested a lively discussion.

"Good morning, Aditi. Good morning, Vaani," Arjun greeted them with a warm smile. "Hope you both had a good sleep last night."

Vaani chuckled. "Yes, yes. But it looks like you didn't sleep well, Arjun. Look at those dark circles under your eyes."

Aditi frowned. "She's right. You look exhausted."

Arjun shrugged. "It was difficult to sleep, but I managed somehow." He gestured toward the bench outside. "You two seem to be having a deep conversation. I'll leave you to it. I'll be sitting outside if you need me."

He smiled and walked away, his footsteps light despite the weight on his mind.

As Arjun disappeared from view, Aditi turned to Vaani. "You know, Vaani? Arjun is actually a nice guy. He never accepts defeat, no matter what life throws at him. Even after losing his parents in an accident and his best friend to that creature, he's still standing strong. That's what makes him resilient."

Vaani's eyes softened. "He truly is remarkable. But you seem to admire him more than just as a friend, don't you?" Aditi's cheeks flushed. She hesitated before speaking. "I think I've fallen for him." Vaani's face lit up. "Oh my God! That's so beautiful. Then why don't you tell him how you feel?"

Aditi's smile faltered. "This isn't the right time, Vaani. There's too much happening." Vaani's brows furrowed. "Then when do you think the right time will come?" Aditi sighed. "I don't know. But I'm leaving it to God. He'll show me the right moment."

Outside, Arjun sat on the bench, the cool morning breeze ruffling his hair. His thoughts were consumed by the mysterious man with the glowing gem.

"Who was he?" Arjun wondered. "Is he the same person who helped us decipher the inscriptions? And if he is, what is his true identity? Is he a divine being or a warrior?"

The questions swirled in his mind, each one more perplexing than the last.

Little did Arjun know that the answers he sought would soon unravel in ways he could never have imagined.

***

The Trials of a Chosen warrior

*"A warrior is not chosen by fate;
he is forged by his trials."*

The afternoon sun filtered through the glass walls of the resort's canteen, casting golden patterns on the polished wooden tables. The smell of freshly prepared meals wafted through the room, blending with the soft murmur of conversations. Plates clinked and glasses clattered, but at a particular table near the window, an uneasy silence loomed.

Arjun sat among his companions — Mohini, Aditi, and Dr. Vaani. The usual gleam in his eyes had dulled, replaced by a faraway gaze. His fingers absently pushed rice around on his plate, and the cheerful chatter that typically echoed from his corner was conspicuously absent. Aditi exchanged a worried glance with Mohini, who leaned forward and gently called, "Arjun?" Her voice carried a hint of concern.

There was no response. Mohini raised her voice slightly, her brows furrowing. "Arjun!"

He blinked, visibly startled. "Wh... what happened?" he stammered, his voice hoarse. "That's what we're asking you," Mohini said, softening her tone. "What's wrong? You seem lost."

Arjun sighed heavily and rubbed his temples. "I'm just... struggling with a wave of questions in my mind. It's not that I can't find answers, but everything seems connected — my dreams, Shreyas's death, everything. And I keep wondering why nature chose me for this responsibility. What makes me eligible for this duty?"

Mohini's eyes softened. "First of all, calm down, Arjun. God tests those who are destined for greatness. Maybe you were born for a purpose. And believe me, you will succeed, beta. You will."

A faint smile tugged at his lips. "As always, thank you, Aunt Mohini. You always know how to lift my spirits."

Dr. Vaani interjected, her voice gentle yet firm. "Arjun, we were planning to go to Suraj Tal today as the old man suggested, but I think you need some rest. Meditation might help calm your thoughts. Try it before sleeping tonight. It'll help you get some peace."

Arjun nodded. "Hmm... okay. I'll do that."

The sky was a deep indigo, with stars scattered like diamonds across a velvet canvas. The cool breeze from the nearby mountains whispered through the trees. Inside his room, Arjun sat cross-legged on his bed, the dim light of a bedside lamp casting long shadows on the walls.

He closed his eyes, inhaling deeply. Memories of his martial arts training in Bombay resurfaced. Meditation had always been his refuge, a place where he found clarity. But tonight was different. No matter how hard he tried, his mind refused to quiet down.

Frustration gnawed at him. "Why can't I go deeper?" he thought.

The moment that thought crossed his mind, a strange warmth spread through his body. A sudden pull, as though invisible hands were guiding him, made him shudder. His breathing slowed, and the world around him faded.

When Arjun opened his eyes, he was no longer in his room. He stood at the entrance of a magnificent passage illuminated by a radiant golden light. The air was thick with the fragrance of celestial flowers that bloomed in vibrant hues, unlike anything found on Earth. Their petals shimmered like gems, and their fragrance was intoxicating.

The floor beneath his feet was made of white marble, smooth and cool to the touch, etched with intricate patterns that pulsed with a soft glow. On either side of the passage, ethereal streams of water flowed, their surfaces reflecting the light of a thousand stars.

Arjun's footsteps echoed as he walked, his heart pounding with a mix of awe and trepidation. The walls of the passage were adorned with carvings depicting the tales of gods and sages, their stories coming alive with every step he took.

After what felt like an eternity, he reached a grand staircase spiraling upwards. The steps gleamed like polished gold, and a faint, melodious chant echoed from above. Without hesitation, Arjun began his ascent.

At the top of the staircase, Arjun entered a vast hall that seemed to stretch beyond the limits of imagination. Pillars of crystalline light supported a ceiling that shimmered like the night sky. The floor was a mosaic of precious stones, each tile radiating divine energy.

In the center of the hall stood a figure bathed in an extraordinary beam of light. The being had four hands — one holding a Kamandalu filled with divine water, another clutching a Rudraksha mala, the third carrying Vedam, the sacred book of knowledge, and the fourth extended in a gesture of blessing.

The radiance surrounding the figure was blinding yet comforting. Arjun instinctively bowed, his voice trembling with reverence. "Oh Lord, thank you for granting me the privilege of your presence. Please help me with my questions. Who am I? What is my purpose? Why did mother nature choose me to end the terror of darkness? Why did my dreams pull me here to Shimla?"

The being smiled benevolently. "I am Jagatpita Brahma, the

creator of the universe. Welcome to Devaloka, my son."

Arjun's heart raced as Brahma's words echoed through the hall.

"You are one of my five warrior creations known as the Maharathis. Long ago, Devaloka faced a great peril. To protect it, I created the Maharathis, each endowed with the power of one element of nature. But darkness corrupted their souls, and Lord Shiva cursed them. Their corrupted souls were imprisoned in unknown places on Earth, while their good souls were destined to be reborn as humans."

Brahma's eyes gleamed with wisdom. "You are the Maharathi with the power of the Earth element. The monster wreaking havoc is your corrupted soul that has possessed the body of Sage Muni-Ratnam."

Arjun's breath caught in his throat. "So... that creature is my corrupted side, and I am the good soul of the Earth-elemented Maharathi. But I have more questions. What was the problem that led to this? Where did the dark consciousness come from? And where are the other Maharathis?"

Brahma's voice was calm yet firm. "There is a time for everything, my son. As time passes, you will find these answers. Your duty now is to defeat this creature and find the remaining Maharathis."

"But how can I find them? I don't know where they are or what their identities are," Arjun pressed. Brahma's lips curved into a reassuring smile. "You have a mystical five-arrowed star symbol on your hand, don't you?"

Arjun raised his hand, revealing the faint glow of the symbol etched on his skin. "Yes, I have it." "This symbol will guide you to them," Brahma said.

Arjun's voice wavered. "Oh Brahma, you are the god. Please help me fulfill this duty."

Brahma's expression grew solemn. "My role is to show you

the path. Walking on it is your responsibility."

Arjun took a deep breath, determination flickering in his eyes. "Thank you, Lord Brahma, for showing me the way."

"Believe in yourself, my son, and make righteous decisions," Brahma advised.

The divine light faded, and Arjun found himself back in his room. His breathing was steady, and his mind was clear. He felt a newfound sense of purpose coursing through his veins.

"I obey your guidance, Lord Brahma," he whispered, his voice filled with conviction.

The night was serene, but within Arjun, a storm of courage and determination raged. The path was set, and he was ready to walk it. The battle against darkness had just begun.

***

The Passage of Quests

"Each step forward is a step into the unknown, where courage is the only guide."

The next day dawned crisp and clear. The morning light filtered through the dense forest canopy as Arjun, Aditi, and Vaani finished their lunch near the campsite.

Determined not to waste any time, they packed their essentials and set off for Suraj Tal near Gandharva Waterfalls, guided by the cryptic instructions of the old sage.

The journey was invigorating, with towering trees flanking the narrow dirt path that wound through thick vegetation. Sunlight played hide-and-seek through the leafy canopy, casting dappled patterns on the forest floor. Birdsong filled the air, accompanied by the occasional rustle of leaves as wild creatures darted out of sight. The earthy scent of moss and damp soil permeated the air.

As they trekked deeper into the wilderness, the rhythmic roar of Gandharva Waterfalls grew louder, like a giant's heartbeat echoing through the mountains. The lake's shimmering surface appeared in the distance, framed by majestic cliffs and veils of cascading water.

"We're finally here," Vaani said, wiping sweat from her brow. Her voice carried both excitement and fatigue.

The tranquil beauty of Suraj Tal was breathtaking. The lake, nestled between rugged mountains, gleamed like a sapphire under the midday sun. Crystal-clear waters mirrored the lush greenery and snow-kissed peaks, creating a mesmerizing panorama. Mist from the distant waterfalls hung in the air, adding an ethereal touch to the landscape.

Despite the serenity, tension hung heavy among the group as they scanned the area for any sign of the hidden weapon.

"There's nothing here," Vaani declared, frustration evident in her voice. "I think that old man fooled us. Let's go back and find him."

"Wait," Arjun said, stepping forward. "I don't think he was lying. If he wanted to trick us, he would have taken something in return—money, food, or anything else. But he didn't."

Aditi, who had been silently observing the lake, interjected, "Can I say something?"

"Go ahead," Arjun encouraged.

"I've seen a lot of adventure movies," Aditi began confidently, "and I'm pretty sure there's something hidden here. Don't you think this weapon must have been concealed with some kind of mechanism?"

Arjun frowned. "That sounds logical, but I don't see anything unusual."

"Trust me," Aditi insisted. "If Ashwatthama wanted to hide it from the world, he would have used some mechanism. Maybe it's invisible to the naked eye."

Just as she finished speaking, her sharp eyes caught something unusual near the center of the lake—a stone tile barely breaching the water's surface.

"Look!" Aditi exclaimed, pointing. "There's a tile in the center."

Arjun and Vaani squinted in the direction she was pointing.

"You're right," Vaani confirmed. "It's partially submerged but visible." "Look closer," Aditi urged. "There's a square-shaped cut on the tile, and I think I see a lotus design."

Arjun's heart raced. "In my vision, I saw a giant lotus

cradling the weapon. Maybe this is connected." "I think you're onto something," Aditi agreed. "But how do we reach it?"

Vaani picked up a small stone and flung it toward the tile. The splash disrupted the lake's calm surface, but nothing happened initially.

Just as they were about to dismiss the idea, the ground beneath their feet trembled. From behind them, two mirror-like stones emerged from the earth, shimmering in the sunlight. Another pair rose on the opposite side of the river. The water around the tile churned violently, and the stone emerged fully, revealing a gleaming diamond embedded in its center.

The crew stood speechless, mesmerized by the dazzling gem.

"Aditi, you're incredible!" Arjun exclaimed, his face lighting up with excitement. Unable to contain his joy, he hugged her. Vaani cleared her throat dramatically. "Ahem."

They pulled apart, blushing furiously.

Returning to the task at hand, Arjun observed the mirror-like structures. "These mirrors are reflecting sunlight toward the diamond, but the two behind us aren't aligned. We need to adjust them so that they all direct light to the diamond."

He approached one of the stones and tried to move it, but it wouldn't budge.

"We'll need to work together," Arjun said. The trio pushed with all their strength, but the stone remained immovable.

"One more try," Arjun urged. As they strained against the stone, he subconsciously uttered, "Jai Mahakal!"

Miraculously, the stone shifted into place. "Mahakal really listens," Vaani whispered in awe.

They repeated the process with the other stone until all four mirrors directed sunlight onto the diamond. The moment the last ray converged, the earth shook violently. Two colossal stone walls rose from the lake, blocking the waterfall's flow. As the water receded, a hidden compartment was revealed, along with a staircase leading into the depths.

"This must be Ashwatthama's mechanism to protect the weapon," Arjun speculated.

Aditi's voice trembled with excitement. "Looks like that staircase leads to the weapon."

Arjun took a deep breath and stepped onto the staircase. As Vaani tried to follow, the step beneath her feet crumbled.

She gasped, flailing for balance, but Aditi grabbed her just in time.

"Be careful!" Arjun warned. "It looks like only one person can enter at a time."

He descended alone, the air growing colder with each step. The walls of the secret chamber were carved from ancient stone and adorned with intricate patterns.

Golden ornaments and treasures gleamed in the dim light, but a foreboding inscription caught his attention:

"What is visible may not be real. Beware of illusions."

Arjun's senses went on high alert. As he advanced cautiously, a sudden voice echoed through the chamber.

"यद त्वं इदं काय समाप्तं न कुयाः, तह वषाणुगन्धेन हतः भवष्यस ।"

If you do not complete this quest, you will perish from poisonous gas."

Startled, Arjun turned to see a bat fluttering before him.

"O bat," Arjun asked, "what kind of quest must I complete?" "You must answer my questions correctly," the bat declared. "Only then will you be allowed to proceed."

"I'm ready," Arjun said confidently.

Question 1: "What is more important — to follow Dharma (righteousness) or to fulfill one's personal desires? Provide an example to support your answer."

Arjun answered without hesitation. "Dharma must always

come before personal desires. Desires are fleeting and selfish, but Dharma sustains society and one's inner peace.

Lord Rama, for instance, chose exile to uphold his father's vow, sacrificing his personal desire to rule Ayodhya. By choosing Dharma, he earned eternal respect."

"Impressive," the bat acknowledged. "Next question: If a tree stands still and silent throughout its life, why is it still considered one of the greatest givers in nature?"

"The tree speaks through its actions," Arjun explained. "It offers shade, fruits, wood, and purifies the air. Its life is a lesson in selfless service. True greatness lies in giving without seeking praise."

"Indeed," the bat agreed. "Now for the third question: If you have two paths—one long but righteous, and another short but deceitful—which would you choose and why?"

"I would choose the long but righteous path," Arjun declared. "Deception may bring temporary success but leads to guilt and downfall. The righteous path may be arduous, but it brings lasting peace and honor."

The bat's eyes gleamed. "Final question: Imagine you're leading a group on a journey. A fierce storm strikes with no shelter in sight. What will you do?"

Arjun pondered deeply. "I will lead them to higher ground, look for natural shelters, or organize the group to build a temporary shelter. Courage and calmness will be my tools to protect them."

As Arjun finished, the bat emitted a radiant beam of light and transformed into a beautiful fairy.

"Thank you, Arjun," she said gratefully. "I was once Hrishika, a disciple of Guru Dronacharya. Cursed to be a bat, I was trapped here until someone answered these questions. You have freed me. I will aid you in the future. Farewell."

With that, she disappeared into the light.

Arjun, though happy to have freed the fairy, steeled himself for the journey ahead. Would he finally find the hidden weapon?

***

The Prestigious achievement

"Glory is not in reaching the end, but in conquering the impossible."

The corridor gleamed under the faint luminescence of ancient carvings, glistening like forgotten constellations. Arjun moved further, his heart filled with a strange sense of satisfaction after freeing a long-captive soul. His footsteps echoed through the passage, reverberating off the damp stone walls.

However, as he entered a new compartment, his gaze locked onto a massive glass wall holding back a swirling mass of water, shimmering like liquid sapphire. The sight was surreal—nature confined by ancient magic. Just ahead, a gate stood open, beckoning him forward.

He approached cautiously, heart pounding with curiosity and apprehension. As soon as he reached the threshold and tried to step through, a sudden jolt of energy surged through him.

"Ah!" Arjun yelped, stumbling backward and falling to the cold stone floor. Pain seared through his body. "What was that?"

When he looked up again, the gate had sealed itself shut. Rising from the ground in front of it were four stone pedestals, each now holding a statue of an ancient animal. The carvings were intricate, as though crafted by hands blessed by the gods.

Arjun's eyes widened at the sight: a Vanara with a fierce yet loyal expression, a seven-headed snake coiled in divine elegance, Airavat with its majestic presence, and a white bull adorned with four massive horns.

Four grand pillars stood at the corners of the room, each with a hollow gap in the middle.

Suddenly, a voice, raspy yet commanding, echoed through the chamber. Arjun froze, searching for the source. Without warning, an invisible weight landed on his shoulders, making him stumble.

"मम नाम बेतालः। अहं द्वारस्य रक्षकः। यान चत्वारः प्रतमा यः त्वं पुरतः पश्यस, तान प्रतमा द्वारं उद्घाटयतुं कुजिकाः। त्वं एतान प्रतमाः स्तम्भानां उचते छद्रे स्थापय। यद् तत् सम्यक् कुयाः, तह अहं त्वां अग्रे गन्तुं अनुमोदयाम। अन्यथा अहं त्वां भोजनं करष्याम," the voice declared.

Arjun flinched, not understanding the words. A moment later, the entity spoke again, this time in a language he could comprehend.

"My name is Betal. I am the keeper of the gate. The four statues you see in front of you are the keys to open the door. You must place them correctly in the gaps of the pillars. If you succeed, I will allow you to pass. If not, I shall make you my food."

A chill ran down Arjun's spine as he realized the weight on his back was none other than a Betal—an elusive creature from ancient legends. Arjun had grown up fascinated by the tales of Vikram and Betal, but never in his wildest dreams had he imagined encountering one.

Betal's sharp laugh echoed through the chamber. Arjun knew he had no choice but to solve the riddle. He examined the pillars closely, noting the inscriptions etched into each.

1. I am known for my loyalty and strength, A devotee who crossed the ocean's length. With a mighty leap, I served my lord, Who am I in this ancient accord?
   Arjun immediately recognized the description—it was Hanuman, the Vanara who served Lord Rama.

2. I hold the worlds with grace divine, On me, the preserver chooses to recline. Seven heads I bear, coiled in power, Who am I in this celestial tower?
   The answer was clear—Sheshnag, the divine serpent.
3. I am white and majestic, strong and bold, Born from the churned ocean of gold. A thunderous roar I make in the skies, Indra's trusted steed, I rise.
   This was none other than Airavat, the mighty elephant.
4. Guarding my lord with a steady gaze, In devotion, I spend my days. A gentle bull, pure and wise, Who am I beneath Shiva's skies?
   Nandi, Lord Shiva's devoted bull, was the answer.

Arjun carefully lifted the first statue—the Vanara—and approached the pillar marked by the first riddle. He placed it in the gap, but nothing happened.

"Wrong!" Betal cackled. "Try again, fool!"

Sweat trickled down Arjun's brow. He analyzed the pillar again, realizing his mistake. The markings on the base hinted at a specific alignment. Adjusting the statue, he heard a faint click. Success.

One by one, he repeated the process, enduring several false placements and Betal's taunts. After what felt like an eternity, all four statues were correctly aligned.

The ground trembled, and the gate slowly slid open with a grinding sound. Betal let out a disgruntled huff before vanishing from Arjun's shoulders.

"You've proven yourself worthy, mortal," Betal's voice echoed faintly.

Arjun exhaled in relief, his body aching from the ordeal.

Beyond the gate, a swirling blue portal shimmered, its surface rippling like disturbed water. Strange, eerie sounds emanated from it, sending shivers down Arjun's spine.

Taking a deep breath, he stepped through.

The sensation was indescribable—his body felt weightless, his senses overwhelmed by a rush of colors and sounds. When he emerged on the other side, his breath caught in his throat.

A vast floating island stretched before him, suspended in the sky like a divine realm. Lush greenery covered the landscape, with trees that glimmered as though their leaves were crafted from emeralds. Streams of golden light flowed through the air, and in the center of it all was a magnificent lotus, its petals radiating a brilliant green shimmer.

Towering spruce-like trees surrounded the lotus, their trunks thick and ancient. The air was fragrant with the scent of unknown blossoms, and the sky above was a mesmerizing shade of indigo.

A stone bridge connected the portal to the floating island. Arjun crossed it, marveling at the ethereal beauty around him.

As he reached the island, a thunderous roar echoed through the air. Arjun's heart raced. From atop the grand lotus, a figure leaped down, landing with a ground-shaking thud.

It was a Kimpurush—a majestic being with the body of a man and the head of a white tiger. In its hand, it held a gleaming green bow, and a quiver of arrows rested on its back.

Arjun's eyes widened in disbelief. "A Kimpurush? This creature was part of my research! A tiger-headed being with unmatched combat skills."

The Kimpurush's golden eyes gleamed with challenge. "You are incredibly knowledgeable, mortal. But knowledge alone is not enough. Let's see if you are a true warrior."

With a wave of its hand, a spear materialized in Arjun's grasp. The weapon gleamed menacingly, its blade sharp enough to slice through stone.

Arjun took a defensive stance, his martial arts training kicking in. The Kimpurush notched an arrow and fired with lightning speed. Arjun dodged, the arrow grazing his arm.

The battle was fierce and unrelenting. Arjun's spear clashed against the Kimpurush's arrows, sparks flying with every impact. The Kimpurush moved with feline agility, leaping and attacking from unexpected angles.

In the heat of the fight, Arjun's spear accidentally struck a massive tree. It began to topple, its branches cracking like thunder.

The Kimpurush was directly in its path. Without thinking, Arjun lunged forward, shoving the Kimpurush out of harm's way. The tree crashed onto Arjun instead, pinning him to the ground. Pain shot through his body, but he gritted his teeth, refusing to cry out. The Kimpurush's eyes softened. With a wave of its hand, the tree lifted and floated away.

"You have proven yourself, young warrior," the Kimpurush said solemnly. "Not only are you fierce in battle, but you possess a heart of compassion. The divine blesses such a soul."

The Kimpurush approached the grand lotus and lifted a beautiful bone sword from its heart. The weapon shimmered with divine energy.

"You are the true owner of this weapon, Arjun. Take it. Also take my Bow and Arrows in the form of my blessings. All the very best."

As the Kimpurush vanished into the air, Arjun held the sword tightly, tears welling in his eyes.

"I've cried these many days... but it's time for you to cry, Brahmarakshas."

He had finally achieved the weapon. But would it be enough to defeat the creature that awaited him?

***

The Final Confrontation

"All battles lead to this moment—
the clash of fate, will, and destiny."

The island trembled violently beneath Arjun's feet as he prepared to leave Amarlok. A sudden quake threatened to throw him off balance, and a golden light flared behind him. Startled, Arjun turned to see a small treasure box floating in midair, gleaming with divine brilliance. His heart raced as chills crept down his spine.

"A treasure box? This... this was in my dream." He whispered, trembling.

The box floated closer, and Arjun carefully opened it.

Inside lay a radiant yellow gemstone, pulsating with an ethereal glow. Before he could comprehend its significance, a powerful voice echoed from above.

"Remember, this bone sword will only unleash its full power on Amavasya, the new moon night and it can be used only one time on someone . After the duty is over it will vanish in the air," the voice declared. "My blessings are with you, child."

Arjun immediately recognized the commanding tone—it was Jagatpita Brahma himself. "Thank you, my lord," he whispered reverently. Assured by the divine message, Arjun gripped the bone sword tightly and stepped through the portal, leaving Amarlok behind.

The forest was shrouded in an eerie silence, broken only by the crackling campfire where Aditi and Vaani anxiously awaited Arjun's return. The night air was thick with tension.

"I hope Arjun returns soon," Aditi said, her voice laced with worry.

"He will," Vaani reassured her. "He promised to end this terror."

Suddenly, a guttural growl echoed through the woods, freezing them in place. The ground vibrated as heavy footsteps approached. The shadows shifted, and from the depths of the forest emerged a grotesque creature.

Its glowing yellow eyes gleamed with malevolence. Massive horns, twisted like a deer's, jutted from its head. Its body was covered in matted fur stained with blood, and its claws dripped with a thick greenish liquid. A foul stench permeated the air. Its jagged teeth glinted under the pale moonlight.

Aditi's knees buckled as a wave of fear washed over her. The creature's terrifying aura was overwhelming.

"Aditi! Wake up! Please!" Vaani screamed, shaking her friend.

The creature let out a deafening howl and lunged at them, its claws poised to strike. Vaani braced herself for the inevitable, but a sudden green light illuminated the forest. Arjun appeared, his bone sword gleaming in the darkness.

With a swift movement, he nocked an arrow and released it. The arrow struck the creature with immense force, knocking it back.

The beast roared in rage and charged at Arjun once more. Arjun set another arrow aflame using the campfire and shot it at the creature. But it dodged with unnatural agility and leaped at him.

Just as the beast was about to pounce, a powerful punch sent it flying. Arjun turned in shock to see the same old man who had guided them earlier.

"Give me the box!" the old man commanded.

Arjun handed him the treasure box. The old man opened

it, retrieved the yellow gemstone, and removed the bandage from his forehead. He pressed the gemstone onto a scarred wound on his forehead.

A blinding light enveloped him. His dark, weathered skin turned radiant white. His hunched back straightened, and his frail body became muscular and imposing. His eyes glowed with divine brilliance.

Arjun's breath caught in his throat. "Who... who are you?"

The man's voice thundered through the forest. "I am Dronacharyaputra Ashwathama! Sent by Jagatpita Brahma to aid you in this battle against darkness."

Ashwathama's presence was overwhelming. The air around him shimmered with divine energy.

"Young warrior, you have shown great courage. Now, it's your duty to end this terrifying beast," Ashwathama declared.

He ran his hand over Aditi's head which made her awake.

All eyes were on him. Arjun took a deep breath before addressing the figure standing before them.

"I had my doubts, but now they are finally clarified—I was truly blessed with the guidance of a figure from the Mahabharata. Thank you, Ashwathama, for leading us this far," he said, his voice filled with gratitude.

Ashwathama's gaze softened as he replied, "It was my duty, my child. Perhaps, through this, I have finally found a way out of the torment I have endured for nearly five thousand years. The sins of my past, which I have never been proud of, have at last granted me redemption.

"But this is not where your journey ends. Destroying the creature is only the beginning. You have much farther to go, and your purpose is far from complete. Be careful, for darkness lurks in places you cannot yet see. My blessings will always be with you."

With those final words, Ashwathama turned and

disappeared into the dense foliage, vanishing as mysteriously as he had appeared.

Back at the resort the next morning, Vaani and Aditi could barely contain themselves. They wasted no time in recounting everything to Mohini—the hidden lake, the presence of Ashwathama, and their encounter with the monstrous creature.

Mohini gasped in disbelief. "Oh my God! Does this mean the legends we've heard about the Mahabharata were real? You all actually met Ashwathama? Where is he now?" she asked, eyes wide with astonishment.

Aditi shook her head. "We have no idea. He disappeared into the forest after speaking with us. It was as if the forest swallowed him whole."

Arjun took the opportunity to explain everything—the trials he had faced, the mystical beings he encountered, and the celestial realm of Amarlok that he had visited. He then revealed the ancient bone sword and the bow with its quiver of arrows. The weapons glowed with an ethereal radiance, their power undeniable.

"The majestic voice told me that this weapon will only reveal its true potential on the night of the new moon," Arjun said.

Mohini's expression changed instantly. "The new moon is tonight!"

Arjun's heart pounded in his chest. "What a coincidence!" he exclaimed. "That means tonight is our only chance to end this creature once and for all."

As the sun dipped below the horizon at 6:45 p.m., the group ventured deep into the heart of the forest. They had no concrete idea of where the creature would emerge, but after careful searching, they found a clearing that seemed perfect for the battle.

"Listen carefully," Arjun instructed, his tone firm. "It's

evening now, and the creature could appear at any moment. We must be prepared."

He turned to Aditi and Vaani. "Since we know the monster fears fire, I'll pour kerosene around this area. When the time comes, Aditi, you'll set it ablaze. I will hide in that bush over there, and at the center of the clearing, I'll place a piece of fresh meat drenched in blood to lure it out. Keep your earphones on so we can communicate. Understood?"

"Understood," Vaani nodded.

With everything set, they waited. The hours dragged on, stretching their patience thin. It was close to 1 a.m. when Arjun's voice crackled through the earphones.

"Vaani, Aditi, any movement?"

"Nothing yet, Arjun," Vaani replied.

Then, suddenly, a distant howl echoed through the forest. The air grew thick with tension. Arjun scanned the shadows, gripping his sword tightly. The howling continued, growing louder with each passing minute.

And then, it came.

The monstrous figure emerged from the darkness, its grotesque form illuminated by the moonlight. It sniffed the air, its eyes locking onto the bait. As it moved to claim the meat, Arjun struck first, releasing an arrow that struck the beast's arm. The force of the impact sent it stumbling backward, howling in fury.

Aditi and Vaani sprang from their hiding spots as the beast tore the arrow from its flesh and charged at them. Arjun fired again, each shot stunning the creature momentarily, but it refused to fall.

"Now!" Arjun shouted.

Aditi and Vaani hurled their flaming torches onto the kerosene-soaked ground. In an instant, a wall of fire erupted, encircling the battlefield. The creature snarled, its primal fear evident as it realized it had been trapped.

But it wasn't done yet. With a sudden burst of speed, it lunged at Arjun, striking him with tremendous force. He was thrown across the clearing, crashing into the undergrowth. Dazed, he struggled to his feet, his eyes landing on the bone sword wrapped in cloth.

The moment his fingers closed around the hilt, an unimaginable power surged through him. His entire body was engulfed in a brilliant green aura, his eyes glowing with an intense light. He felt unstoppable.

The beast, now focused on Aditi and Vaani, prepared to strike when a rock slammed into its face. Snarling, it turned to see Arjun standing tall, his transformed presence radiating divine energy.

The creature roared and lunged, but before it could reach him, a glowing rope of pure light materialized from the darkness, wrapping tightly around its body.

"Arjun, now! Strike it down!"

The voice belonged to the fairy he had rescued during his trials.

Without hesitation, Arjun rushed forward, roaring like a lion. He raised the bone sword high and drove it deep into the creature's chest. The beast shrieked in agony, its body convulsing as it began to rise into the sky.

Above them, the clouds shifted, forming the visage of Lord Shiva. From His third eye, a celestial beam of light struck the writhing monster, reducing it to pure energy. The remnants of that energy coalesced into a spectral figure—Muni Ratnam.

The sage's spirit descended, his eyes filled with gratitude.

"Thank you, Arjun, for freeing me from this wretched entity. But you must know—your green aura, the power granted to you by the blade, is the manifestation of the Earth element. This power is now yours to wield."

As the sage spoke, Arjun's clothes transformed into those of an eternal warrior. He clenched his fists, realization dawning upon him.

"The exact elemental power that Lord Brahma spoke of in my past life," he thought.

With a final nod of appreciation, Muni Ratnam's soul ascended into the heavens, vanishing into the breaking dawn.

Victory had been achieved.

As the first light of morning stretched across the sky, the group made their way back to the resort. They had freed Shimla from the terror that had plagued it for so long. But as they walked, Arjun knew the battle was far from over.

There were still shadows lurking, dark entities waiting in the unknown.

And he was not the only one meant to fight them.

There were four more warriors out there—waiting to be found.

Waiting to be awakened.

***

Vedant Phadke

Poet, story writer and aspiring film director

Vedant Phadke, 18-year-old college management student, has several dreams and is working hard to achieve them. He is a poet, story writer and aspiring film maker and budding entrepreneur.

He has written his debut novel "The Epics of Ved Verse – Part 1: Arjun," which was inspired by Indian mythology and historical narratives. It is racy and visually enriching with detailed accounts of nature and the inner workings of the human mind.

Growing up in the picturesque village of Kadoli, he was fascinated by nature and the mythological stories the elders told him. He aspires to be an entrepreneur and produce films that have an impact.

—Rishikesh Bahadur Desai

Senior Assistant Editor, *The Hindu*, Belagavi

www.ingramcontent.com/pod-product-compliance
Lightning Source LLC
Chambersburg PA
CBHW062145160726
48282CB00027B/946
* 9 7 8 8 1 9 8 4 5 1 8 9 7 *